For Jane, who agreed to marry a pirate and didn't even change her mind when she found out I was an illustrator – J.D.

LANDSICKNESS TABLETS

FINEST CUTLASS POLISH

A TEMPLAR BOOK

First published in the UK in hardback
in 2011 by Templar Publishing,
this softback edition published in 2012 by Templar Publishing,
an imprint of The Templar Company Limited,
The Granary, North Street,
Dorking, Surrey, RH4 1DN, UK
www.templarco.co.uk

ISBN 978-1-84877-392-9

Edited by Libby Hamilton and A.J. Wood

Printed in China

The Pirates Next Door

Starring THE JOLLEY-ROGERS

by JONNY DUDDLE

templar publishing

Matilda lived in Dull-on-Sea, a gloomy seaside town – too busy in the summer...

and in winter it shut down.

There weren't too many kids around –
just Tilda on her street.
The lawns were mowed,
the cars were washed,
the hedges trimmed and neat.

The house next door had been for sale
since Tilda was a baby.
She hoped a family would move in
with a girl her age
or maybe...

He had patched-up jeans, an EYEPATCH and a WOODEN-LEGGED dog!

And a PIRATE SHIP with TREASURE CHESTS and barrels full of GROG!

"We're the
JOLLEY-ROGERS!
We'll be anchoring next door.
We've sailed the seven seas
but now we've had
to come ashore."

"I feel a little landsick,
but Mum says it'll pass.
That's my mother over
there, digging up
the grass."

"That's Dad over yonder – the captain of our crew. He likes to shout

OO-ARR!

a lot...

...'coz that's what pirates do."

"Grandpa won't set foot on shore.
He's allergic to dry land.
The last time that he left the ship
the King chopped off his hand!"

"That urchin there's called Nugget. She's a rascal as you'll see. She ain't learnt to fire a cannon yet, but then she's only three."

Next morning, Tilda blurted:

Life's not
BORING
any more!

Isn't it
FANTASTIC
that those pirates
moved next door?

But Mum
and Dad
were not
impressed...

The teacher said Jim should wear SHOES...

and his uniform was wrong.

She wrote a note...

but Jim replied,

I won't be staying long!

We're only 'ere a little while, so Dad can fix our ship. We ain't cut out for life on land – this stay be just a blip.

We are the Jolley-Rogers and we need to be at sea. School's just grand but understand it's a PIRATE's life for me!

After school, a neighbour
came around for cake and tea.
Her name was Mrs Bumble
from number thirty-three.

Miss Pinky
called the council, to see
what they could do.

She didn't live
through two world wars,
to have PIRATES
spoil her view!

Shhh!

Purrr!

Isn't it DISGRACEFUL, on such a lovely street?
You'd think that they would TRY to keep their garden looking neat!

They wear old clothes and scruffy hats.
And I'm told their ships
are full of RATS!

Also cross was Mr Shaw,
the grumpy man at thirty-four.
He liked to read the paper
on his sunlit patio.
But the pirates' ship blocked out
the light, so he said...

THEY'LL HAVE TO GO!

I'd like some PEACE and QUIET, but they're fixing up that boat! Hammering all day and night. That thing will NEVER float!

The two Miss Yates
at eighty-eight,

told everyone who
passed their gate:

"We saw them
grab the POSTMAN.
They made him
walk the plank!
It's lucky he can swim
but we're afraid his
postbag sank."

88

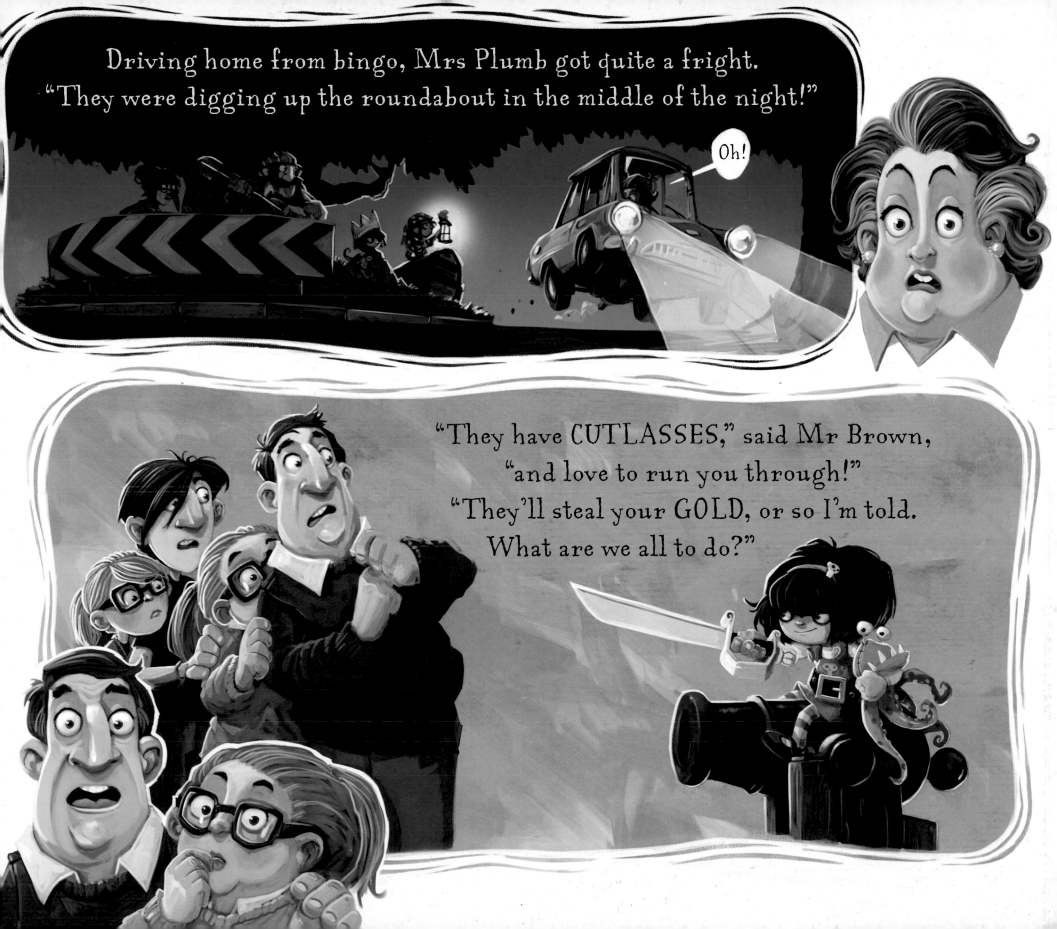

Before you know it, there'll be more – we'll all have pirates lodged next door!
The Jolley-Rogers cannot stay. YOU must make them GO AWAY!

"Whenever we
stop somewhere new,
the neighbours are unkind.
To show them pirates
aren't so bad, we leave
some things behind."

Shhh!

Matilda woke next morning,
puzzled by what Jim had said.
She vowed she'd keep in touch with him
as she struggled out of bed.

Oh, what a SHAME they left!
I didn't say GOODBYE.
They were such a LOVELY family...
I think I'm going to CRY!
Quack!

She opened up her curtains,
as she stretched and had a yawn,
and there, to her amazement,
was a CROSS on every lawn!

After that, the town went on
landlubbing happily.
But Tilda now goes fishing
on the jetty by the sea.
She's waiting for a message
to wash up on the shore
from her very special PIRATE friend –
the one who lived NEXT DOOR.